Heat wave

written by Eileen Spinelli

illustrated by Betsy Lewin

Harcourt, Inc.

Orlando Austin New York
San Diego Toronto London

Requests for permission to make copies of any part of the work
should be submitted online at www.harcourt.com/contact
or mailed to the following address: Permissions Department,
Harcourt, Inc., 6277 Sea Harbor Drive, Orlando, Florida
32887-6777.

www.HarcourtBooks.com

Library of Congress Cataloging-in-Publication Data
Spinelli, Eileen.
Heat wave/Eileen Spinelli; illustrated by Betsy Lewin.
p. cm.
Summary: Abigail, Ralphie, and the other citizens of Lumberville
struggle to endure a week-long heat wave.
[1. Heat—Fiction. 2. City and town life—Fiction.] I. Lewin, Betsy,
ill. II. Title.
PZ7.S7566Hea 2007
[E]—dc22   2005018946
ISBN 978-0152-16779-0

First edition
H G F E D C B A

Printed in Singapore

The illustrations in this book were done with brush and Sumi ink
and Winsor Newton tube watercolors on Strathmore bristol board.
The display and text type was set in Catseye-Medium.
Color separations by Bright Arts Ltd., Hong Kong
Printed and bound by Tien Wah Press, Singapore
This book was printed on totally chlorine-free
Stora Enso Matte paper.
Production supervision by Jane Van Gelder
Designed by Scott Piehl

For Marty Ranft
and Bob Jepsen
and Sid Simon
—Eileen

For Claire Rose Reilly
and Logan Patrick McMurray
—Betsy

SUN SIZZLed. HaiR fRIZZLed.

It was a sweltering day in Lumberville—long before stores, businesses, or homes had air conditioners. Newspaper headlines declared . . .

Pastor Denkins shortened his sermon. The Green Door Restaurant served fruit plates with orange sherbert. Abigail Blue and her little brother, Ralphie, opened a lemonade stand—three cents a glass. On Monday the Palace movie theater closed. It stayed closed for the week.

TueSday was hOtter.

Officer McGinnis soaked all afternoon in a bubble bath. Lottie Mims took four cold showers.

Wednesday was even hOtter.

The Pettibone sisters fanned themselves with magazines and aprons. Mr. and Mrs. Blue found shade where they could. Lottie Mims wore her bathing suit to clean house. Mike Morello, the mailman, tied a wet kerchief around his neck. Abigail and Ralphie forgot about the lemonade and just sold ice.

At five o'clock Mrs. Blue went down to do her cooking on a stove in the cool, dark basement. Mike Morello did no cooking at all.

Thursday was hotter still.

Lottie Mims took a nap with cold tea bags on her eyes. The Pettibone sisters put their perfume and makeup in the icebox. Mr. Blue shaved off his beard and came to supper in his undershirt.

Friday—was it possible?
—was hotter still.

Abigail Blue got her hair cut short in her mother's kitchen barbershop. Ralphie Blue splashed outside in a tin washtub.

Saturday was the hottest day yet.

Butchy Bezwick and Charley Pappas squirted each other with garden hoses and lay on the cool linoleum listening to the radio.

"Take me to the drugstore for an ice-cream soda, please," Abigail Blue begged her father. "Please!"

"Me, too!" piped Ralphie.

In the park most of the kids were playing barefoot. Lottie Mims's cat, Herman, dozed under the porch. Mike Morello's dog, Wags, drooped by the screen door, waiting for a breeze.

Night fell, but not the temperature.

Pastor Denkins took an ice pack to bed. The Pettibone sisters dragged their mattresses to the sleeping porch. Mailman Mike Morello slept on the rooftop. Butchy Bezwick slept on the fire escape. Charley Pappas camped out in his backyard.

At last the Blues, Lottie Mims, and Officer McGinnis left their homes altogether. They carried pillows and quilts to the riverbank.

The mayor of Lumberville passed out Popsicles and political flyers. Officer McGinnis played his harmonica. The river whispered. Stars twinkled. The moon cast a soft, silvery light.

Some people fell asleep in their street clothes.
Some in nightshirts.
Some in pajamas.

Lottie Mims lay very still. Abigail Blue tossed and turned. Ralphie Blue snored. Mr. Blue stuck cotton in his ears.

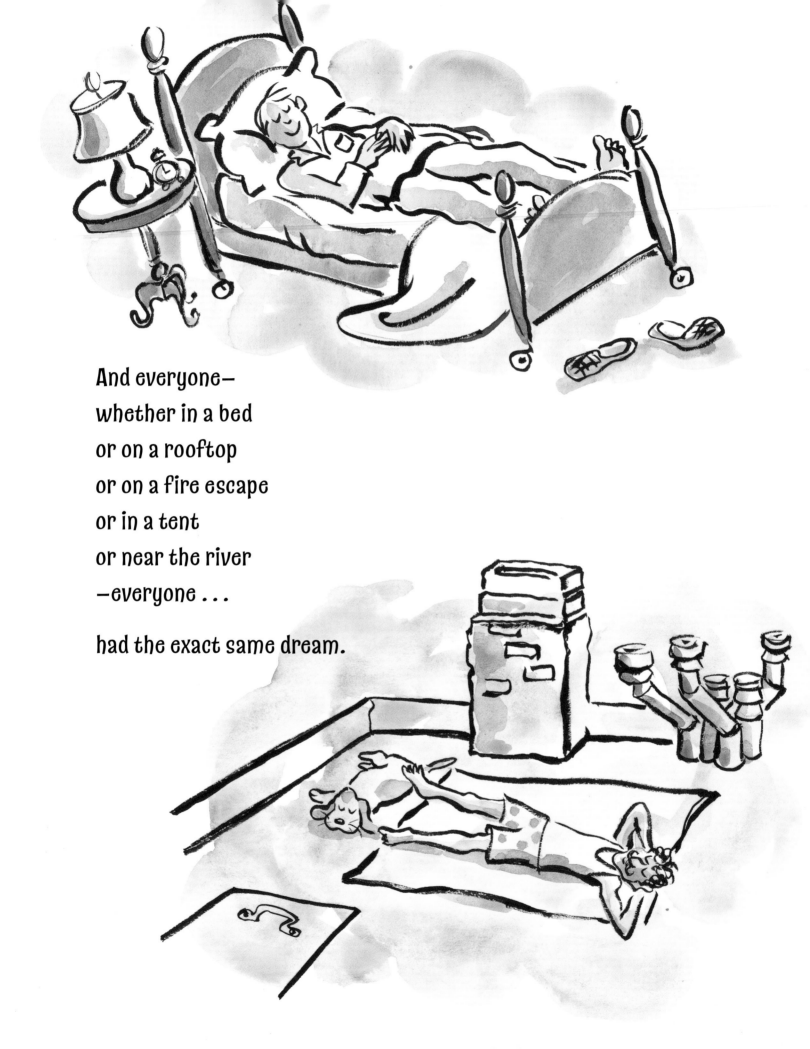

And everyone—
whether in a bed
or on a rooftop
or on a fire escape
or in a tent
or near the river
—everyone . . .

had the exact same dream.